Anne Rooney does not eat meat, in case the taste of blood

appealing.

When not writing books she haunts the cemeteries and catacombs of Paris and Venice and raises non-vampiric daughters and chickens in Cambridge. She studied at a haunted college and her first car was a haunted van; the undead hold no fears for her.

With thanks to Kate and Hannah Frew, Mary Hoffman, Shahrukh Husain, Dr Alison Cluroe (Addenbrooke's Hospital) and Steve Rooney.

Dead on Arrival

by Anne Rooney
www.annerooney.co.uk

Published by Ransom Publishing Ltd.
Radley House, 8 St. Cross Road, Winchester, Hants.
SO23 9HX, UK
www.ransom.co.uk

ISBN 978 184167 301 1
First published in 2012

A CIP catalogue record of this book is available from the British Library.

Dead on Arrival

ANNE ROONEY

The Story So Far

Hungary, August ...

Juliette, Omar, Finn, Ruby and Alistair find a dead body in the forest ...

... Twenty-four hours later, they tie the murderer, Ava, to a tree, as one by one they fall sick ...

... When they wake, they are vampires, and that murderer looks rather appealing ...

... Mysterious nobleman Ignace, 400 years old and more sophisticated than is good for him, prevents them snacking on her ...

... But that dead body isn't as dead as it looked ...

... They go to Ignace's castle for a crash-course in being a modern vampire.

And so their adventures begin.

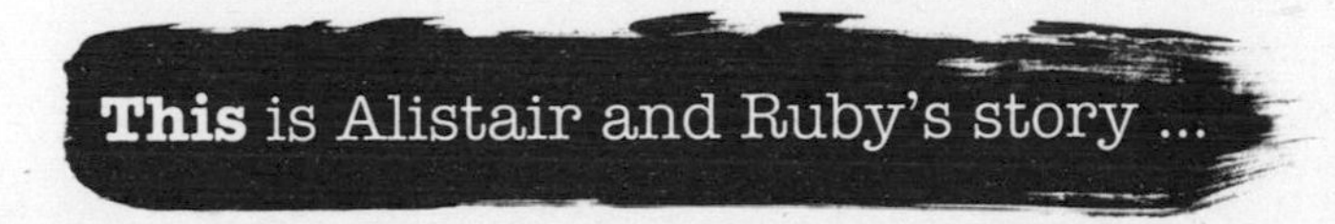

One

'He's been here all night. Stone cold – no pulse,' the paramedic said, looking at Alistair's body slumped in the road, his head slammed against the kerb.

'There's not much blood,' he said. 'I guess the rest must have washed away in the rain.'

The woman who had called the ambulance stood on the footpath with both hands raised to her mouth. Two paramedics loaded Alistair's body onto a stretcher and pulled the blanket over his head. A police officer took a statement from the woman, while her dog tugged at its leash and sniffed his boots.

The ambulance drove off, without sirens or lights.

* * * * *

Ruby tried her brother's mobile again and again, but it went to voicemail every time. *It must be out of battery,* she thought. It was so unlike Alistair – he always kept his phone charged. He'd gone to Ben's for the night. She wished she had Ben's number.

Ruby made toast and flicked the TV on, trying to distract herself. She was alone in the house.

By eleven, she couldn't stand it any more. The rain started again, and was falling hard by the time she passed the police tape at the end of Ben's road. She hurried on, head down. Ben answered the door in his dressing gown. He was surprised to see her.

'Alistair? He didn't come. I thought he'd just changed his mind,' Ben said.

Ruby's mouth was suddenly dry.

'No. No, he really wanted to come,' she said.

'Come in a minute.' Ben held the door open for her.

* * * * *

Alistair opened his eyes. He was cold. And he was on some kind of trolley. Panic rose in his throat like bile, and his head hurt. A bright light from a tube shone in his eyes. He couldn't move his head without it hurting.

Hospital, he thought. *I must be in hospital. I hurt. Hurt people go to hospital.*

He tried to speak, but his mouth wouldn't work. People moved around the room, but he couldn't see them. He wanted to call to them. How many were there? Two? Three? Their voices sounded fuzzy at first, but then words started to creep out of the mumbling:

'Looks like a hit and run ... no ID ... doesn't match any missing persons ... '

His eyes closed again, and he drifted somewhere else. Somewhere he couldn't hear the voices, but somewhere his head still hurt.

When he next opened his eyes the room was silent. He hurt all over. He touched his head. His fingers felt the edges of a cut and he winced. The room was cold. The arm he had lifted to his head was bare – no wonder he was cold. He was naked. Why?

He struggled to remember where he was and what had happened. He had gone to see Ben. They were going to play on the Xbox all night. It had been dark and rainy.

... Now he remembered. Car headlights coming round the corner, just as he stepped off the kerb. Trying to step back, but twisting his ankle and the car still coming. He didn't remember it hitting him, or being hurt. But here he was, so he must have been hit.

He pushed himself up on one elbow. There was a sheet over him, but no blankets. He'd expected to see a hospital ward, but that wasn't what he saw. He was in a room with bare trolleys, not beds. The end wall was covered in large metal handles. And there were no doctors or nurses. There was someone on the next trolley – an old woman. She had her eyes shut.

She must be asleep, he thought. *I'll be quiet.*

His clothes weren't near his trolley. There wasn't a chair, or a table for his things, or a TV. There wasn't even a button to push to make the nurse come. It was nothing like the hospitals he'd seen on TV. Maybe because he mostly watched American hospital programmes – perhaps they were very different in England.

Further along the room there was a desk with a computer on it and a jumper draped over the back of the desk chair. Alistair didn't like to take someone else's things, but he was so cold. *I'll bring it back,* he thought. *I just need it until I find my clothes.*

The jumper was very big, and came almost to his knees.

He glanced at the computer screen. There was a photo of his face, with his eyes closed and a form, partly filled in. The fields for his name and age were blank. He was about to fill them in, but thought he'd better not touch it.

And then he saw the notes under his photo: 'Unidentified white male; dead on arrival. Hit and run. Criminal investigation.'

Two

How do you feel when you're dead? Surely not the same as before. Surely his head shouldn't be hurting if he was dead? *I don't want to be dead,* Alistair thought. *Am I dead?*

It was hard to tell – he hadn't been dead before, so how would he know?

If he didn't fill in his name on the computer, perhaps he wouldn't be dead. Perhaps someone else would be dead, or perhaps no one would be. What if he filled in someone else's name? Would they be dead?

He looked around the room. No wonder it didn't look like a hospital ward. The other people in the room were dead: the old lady who wasn't moving, and a shape under a sheet. It was a morgue – he was in a morgue. That wasn't good for someone who didn't want to be dead.

He had seen on *CSI* what happens to dead people in a morgue – how scientists make a Y-shaped cut from the person's shoulders to their groin and take the insides out.

His palms went sweaty with panic. He had to get out of the morgue before someone came with big knives to cut him open.

Alistair's legs didn't want to move, but he forced them to. He stumbled to the door, but something flapped about near his foot. He looked down. There was a label on his toe. He'd seen that on TV, too. They put a label on the toe of each dead person so they don't get the bodies mixed up.

He stooped to pull it off, but it was fixed with a plastic band like a cable tie. He had to hop on one foot and cut it off with scissors from the desk. He hid it in the bottom of the bin in case he got into trouble for being alive and taking it off.

He opened the door carefully, just enough to peek out. A hospital man in green scrubs was walking towards him. Alistair held the door still until the man had gone, then he looked in both directions.

To the left an arrow pointed to 'Food Court'. He'd been there with Ben once when Ben had had an operation. They'd gone to get pizza because Ben didn't like the hospital food. Ben had worn his pyjamas and there were other people there in dressing gowns.

Perhaps no one would notice Alistair there. Perhaps no one would know he was supposed to be dead.

* * * * *

Ruby's stomach turned over and over. When Alistair hadn't turned up, Ben had texted him, but got no answer. He just thought Alistair had changed his mind, or forgotten.

'But he doesn't!' Ruby cried. 'You know he doesn't just change his mind or forget. Why didn't you call me?'

Even as she said it, she knew it was unfair to blame Ben. Ben stared past her at the wall.

'What should we do?' he asked. 'Shall we call the police?'

Ruby was about to say 'yes, call them,' but then she was unsure. You can't just phone the police and say a vampire is missing.

She knew she wouldn't be able to get hold of their mum. Should she call their vampire mentor, Florence? After they became vampires in Hungary, Ignace had assigned Florence to look after them both, as they each got used to being a vampire.

Maybe she *should* call Florence, Ruby thought. If Alistair didn't have any ProVamp capsules with him, then soon he would hunger for blood. But she couldn't tell Ben – they weren't allowed to tell people they were vampires.

'Um, no, not the police,' she said. 'Maybe he got mixed up. Perhaps he went to Jake's instead.' It sounded lame and she knew it.

'Let me know, right?' Ben said, as he let her out.

Ruby hugged her arms around her in the cold. At the end of the road she stopped. The police tape. She'd thought nothing of it on the way to Ben's house, but now it was scary.

She asked an officer taking photos what had happened.

'Hit and run,' he said.

'Who?'

'Some kid.' He sounded annoyed, as though he didn't like people asking about accidents.

Ruby's heart lurched.

'My brother – he's missing,' she said. 'What did the kid look like?'

The officer suddenly took an interest.

'I don't know, I didn't see him. They took him to the hospital. You should go there.'

Ruby would have to go home, get money, wait for a bus. It was impossible that something so important, so urgent, should have to be done in the same way as everything else – as slowly as if she wanted to go shopping.

'Can't you take me?'

'No, I have work to do here. Don't you have parents?'

Not what you'd really call parents, Ruby thought.

'Yeah, I'll get a lift.'

She went home to get bus money.

Three

At the hospital, Ruby went straight to A&E – Accident and Emergency – where they took people who came in by ambulance. She spoke to the nurse at reception.

'No trace, sorry,' the nurse said. 'Have you reported him missing? He's seventeen? Couldn't he just be at a friend's house? Seventeen-year-old boys, they're not good at keeping in touch. Perhaps he had a bit to drink?'

The nurse was trying to be kind, but it didn't help. She didn't know Alistair.

'He's not like other boys,' Ruby said. She didn't want to go into the ways Alistair was different – him being Asperger's, and a vampire.

At that moment a doctor walked past the check-in desk. He half-heard, stopped, and called the nurse over. Ruby watched the woman's face change.

'You're looking for your brother?' the doctor asked.

Ruby nodded.

'What does he look like?'

Ruby described him, trying to remember what he was wearing. She searched the doctor's face for clues, but he let nothing slip. He just asked her to wait.

It was five minutes before he came back, his face serious. He and a nurse led her into a side room.

'Is anyone with you?' the doctor asked. Ruby shook her head.

'Anyone at home we can call?' She shook her head again.

'A young man was brought in earlier today who had been involved in a hit-and-run accident. We haven't been able to identify him.'

'Is he OK?' Ruby asked, but she knew the answer already.

'I'm afraid not. He was dead on arrival.'

Ruby clasped her hands together so tightly her

fingers turned white.

'It might not be my brother.'

'No, it might not. But I think you should be prepared for the worst. Would you like to see his possessions?'

'His possessions?'

'His clothes and so on.'

'You mean he's not wearing his clothes?' Ruby asked.

The nurse laid a hand on Ruby's arm.

'His clothes have been removed. That's usual. We have to work out why someone has died.'

'I have to see him!' Ruby jumped up, suddenly horrified. They couldn't cut him open, do a post-mortem. He might not even be dead.

'Of course you may see him,' the doctor said calmly. 'But are you sure you want to do it alone? How old are you?'

'You haven't started cutting him up, have you?'

'No. Goodness, no.'

'Did you try to revive him?'

Ruby was frantic, but not just for the reasons the doctor and nurse thought. Who knows what harm they would do him if they tried to make his vampire body return to a normal heart rate and breathing?

'There was no hope of reviving him,' the doctor said. 'He was cold. He wasn't breathing, and his heart wasn't beating. He'd been like that for a long time. Many hours.'

'He was hit by a car?' Ruby asked.

'It appears so. I'll arrange for you to see him.' And the doctor left the room.

A few minutes later, he returned, suddenly flustered and alarmed.

'I'm sorry, there'll be a delay. Would you like some tea? Coffee?'

'No, thanks. What's wrong? Where is he?' Hope and panic struggled together in Ruby's mind. The doctor saw it.

'He's been moved. I'll have to find the person who moved him. Please don't be alarmed.'

But how could she not be alarmed?

four

Plenty of people wore T-shirts and slippers in the hospital's Food Court, so Alistair didn't stand out.

There were people with bandages that covered injuries or operation scars. No visible blood anywhere, but he was aware of the smell. It was a metallic thrill in his nose and at the back of his throat – just the first stirrings of that hunger. It pulled his nerves taut, like guitar strings, and already he wanted more of the feeling.

He hadn't had ProVamp since the day before. He needed to go back and look for his clothes, then take his ProVamp. And he wanted his phone. He had to phone Ruby. She would help him – she always did.

He went back towards the morgue, but stopped when he saw a group of people standing by the door leading into the morgue. A security guard spoke into a walkie-talkie, and a woman in a lab coat pointed at the door. Alistair slipped into a side corridor. There was a door open to his right and he went through it into a dark room.

He was in some kind of storeroom, with racks and racks of scrubs – the green outfits surgeons wore. He pulled some down and changed into them quickly, stuffing the jumper behind a stack of boxes. He pulled a green cap over his hair and surgical boots onto his bare feet. Then he slipped out into the corridor and walked as confidently as he could away from the morgue. A nurse held a door open for him; it said 'Staff only'. An ID badge swung against her chest. He didn't have one.

The niggling desire for blood was growing into a real hunger. It was getting hard to think of anything else. He was in a hospital. It was full of people, and some of them must be bleeding. He could taste it in the air. He didn't want to want it, but he did, and the strength of his wanting was growing stronger by the minute.

His feet drew him after the scent of blood, a scent so faint no ordinary person would have been able to tell it was there. But now his keen vampire senses made his awareness of blood as sharp as a shark's, and the scent pulled him through corridors towards A&E. He barely needed to glance around the waiting room to find someone bleeding. But the hunger was not yet so strong that it overpowered him. He knew he couldn't do it here.

Two police officers talked urgently with a nurse sitting at a desk. Alistair backed against the wall, then edged out of the room unseen. Were they looking for him? He was supposed to be dead. Dead people don't walk away. What do they do to dead people who aren't dead? Would they have to kill him? He had no idea.

The terror of what they might do to him was greater than the desire for blood. He hurried away again, back into the maze of corridors. But how long would it be before his hunger for blood grew too strong to ignore?

five

It was not long. The scent of blood dragged Alistair into a ward, between curtains to a bed.

The woman in it was unconscious, or dead. He didn't know which – he didn't even care which. He wrenched a tube from her wrist and pulled her hand to his mouth.

His lips closed around the tiny needle hole on the inside of her wrist. He played his tongue over the skin. It was salty, warm, with the iron tang of blood. He sucked hard, imagining the drops of red on his tongue, and his mouth filled with saliva. But so little came from her, such a tiny hole. It just made his hunger all the worse.

He knew he had to bite her. Though his mind said he shouldn't, every fibre of his body screamed with the need to sink his teeth into her flesh and feel the blood flood into his mouth.

The woman hadn't stirred. He bit into her arm. Her skin, papery and dry, at first dented under the pressure. Then he felt the click as his teeth punctured the skin and sank into flesh. The salty, metal taste swelled in his mouth, and made a noise like the sea in his head.

He sucked with such force that he felt he must

surely drain her.

Heady with the taste of it, he lifted his face. A large greyish-white circle had appeared around an ugly bite mark. It was not what he had expected. He'd seen so many vampire movies. Where were the neat puncture wounds, the two spots of blood? The edges of this wound were ragged, and the line of his tooth marks was uneven. His dentist was right – he needed braces.

But no more blood would come from the woman. He rubbed her arm. Nothing. It didn't glow pink again, as a living arm would. The blood vessels had collapsed under the pressure of his sucking. What would happen now? He still needed more, but it wouldn't come.

He put a hand on the woman's bony chest. It

didn't rise and fall. He felt her neck, longing to feel the promising pulse of blood moving beneath the skin. Nothing. The woman was dead. Had he killed her? Or had she been dead already? Alistair knew he should care, but he didn't. He just wanted more. Why couldn't he suck her dry? He struggled to marshall his thoughts, to work out what to do, but his mind returned only to the flood of red that he needed more than anything in the world.

Think, Alistair. What do you know? How can you work this out? he coaxed himself silently. *CSI. Think back to those CSI episodes. The bodies on the slab are pale, they are grey. Where does the blood go? Down! It goes down! Of course*. But the woman was lying flat, so the blood would be pooling at her back. That wasn't easy to get.

He glanced around. It was hard to see just by the

glow of screens, but it was a hospital, there must be something sharp lying around that he could use.

He couldn't find anything. His head was still swirling with the need for blood. He pulled aside the woman's hospital gown, wrenching the loose back flap from beneath her and exposing flesh that was deep purply-red, plump with the promise of blood.

It was difficult to get his mouth into the right position to bite her, but with his cheek crushed against the trolley he could just manage it. This wasn't like it was in the movies, either. Dracula never had his face mashed against a hospital trolley and his mouth gaping around the buttocks of a smelly old woman. It was disappointing. He'd thought it was going to be cool to be a vampire. This was more like being a junkie.

But he forgot all that in an instant. The woman's skin was thin and burst easily under his teeth this time, like a ripe raspberry. Blood poured into his mouth, flowing around his teeth and over his tongue. He pressed, sucked, drew in so much it made his head light.

It took longer this time to suck out all he could. He wanted to move along her body, bite again, but there was a noise somewhere outside. He raised his head, tilting it to listen, like a wild animal disturbed. Footsteps. He pulled his mouth away quickly.

Somewhere a light turned on. A ghostly glow filled the cubicle and he saw there was not a trace of blood visible on the body. He slipped out. Curtains around another bed shifted as someone behind them moved around. No one saw him leave the ward.

Six

Alistair felt a warm glow from the blood. It was as though every part of his body had been bathed in hot, holiday sun. But he still wanted more. That made it difficult to think.

For nearly an hour he walked the corridors, learning the layout of the hospital. He must not attract attention. He must look as if he knew where he was going, though he didn't.

He followed two nurses to the staff canteen. Most people were talking in groups, but one or two sat alone reading the paper or poking at their phones.

He took a cup of water and sat at a table. No one looked at him. After a while, a young man about his age left his security pass and newspaper on a table and joined a queue. Alistair stood up, brushed past the table so that both things fell to the floor, then picked them up. He returned the paper to the table, but hid the pass in his hand. Outside, he looped the lanyard over his head, turning the photo towards his chest, and strode quickly down the corridor.

He drifted back towards the morgue, but the area was still crowded. There was even a policeman. He walked past quickly, head down, and turned a corner. What were the police doing there? Was it because he had stolen a jumper? He wanted to return it and make them go away.

Suddenly he wanted to see Ruby. She would know what to do. He had no idea how to get home, but he knew it had to be a long way. He had no money for a bus.

Panic twisted Alistair's stomach and he felt suddenly sick and cold. He didn't want this to be happening any more. It wasn't an adventure, it was scary and strange.

All he was allowed to do was be dead, and he couldn't even get that right: he had got himself un-dead and started walking about.

He liked to know what was happening and what would happen next. But now he was stuck walking around a hospital. Eight hundred years, Ignace told him he would live. Eight hundred years walking around a hospital was going to get boring. It was boring already.

* * * * *

The nurse ushered Ruby into another room. It didn't look like a normal hospital room. It had wallpaper and a bowl of flowers, and comfy chairs.

'Where's this?' Ruby asked.

'It's called the mortuary viewing room,' the nurse said. 'It's where we bring the deceased person to be identified or viewed by relatives.'

They waited five minutes, then ten, and still the doctor didn't come back.

'What's happening?' Ruby asked the nurse. 'When can I see my brother?'

The nurse fetched the doctor. His professional calm was gone. He looked worried and flustered as he ran a hand over his balding head.

'I'm sorry,' he said. 'I don't know what's happened – I can't explain it. The body isn't where it should be.'

'Perhaps he's not dead!' Ruby said. 'Perhaps he got better and – '

'No. He was certainly dead. We don't make mistakes like that in a hospital.'

'Well, you obviously make *some* kind of mistakes, if a dead person can go missing,' Ruby snapped.

The doctor spread his fingers.

'I'll see what I can discover.'

Ruby didn't want to wait any longer, but what else could she do? Two policemen arrived, but they walked straight past her into the room she now realised was the morgue. As the door opened, a blast of cold air hit her.

At last, the doctor, the nurse and a policeman led Ruby into another room. Alistair's clothes lay on a table. Blood smeared the shoulder of his grey sweatshirt, and his trainers were wet with mud.

'Are these your brother's clothes?' the doctor asked. Ruby nodded. Tears pricked her eyes. She didn't trust herself to speak.

'And these?' Alistair's things lay in a small plastic

tray. It was impossible that they could look so impersonal, so ordinary. So like – well, just things. His phone was crushed. He wouldn't be happy about that, Ruby thought. And then the tears fell. She so hoped he was alive to be unhappy about it.

'I'm sorry,' the doctor said. 'I have to ask you – can you tell me what these are?'

He pointed to two ProVamp capsules in the tray.

Oh no, thought Ruby. *Wherever he is, he doesn't have ProVamp. How long will he last?*

'Are they a prescribed medication? Can you tell us what they're for?' the doctor asked.

Should she tell them? She looked at the doctor's face, trying to work out what to do.

'Do you know?' he persisted. 'Was he a drug abuser?'

Ruby shook her head.

'OK. Never mind. We'll send them to the lab.'

'He'll need them if he comes back,' she said at last.

'He isn't going to come back,' the nurse said, laying a hand on Ruby's arm. Ruby shook it off.

'He's not dead!' she shouted. 'You've not got his body, have you? Dead people don't just walk off. He's obviously not dead, and you need to find him because he's hurt and he'll need his medicine.'

'What's the medicine for?' the doctor persisted.

'It's for blood,' Ruby said. It was sort of true.

'He had a blood disorder? What did he have?'

Ruby shrugged, pretending not to know. They all looked at the tray of Alistair's belongings.

'Can we take some details from you, please?' the policeman said at last. But then the door opened and another doctor came in.

'There's been an incident on one of the wards. Please come.'

Ruby was left alone with the nurse again.

Seven

Alistair noticed something different about the hospital. The medical people in the corridors were tense and looked around anxiously.

He went to the staff canteen again and stood looking at a noticeboard, listening to the chatter as he drank a cup of water. The police were looking for someone, he heard – someone who did things to dead bodies. Someone who had stolen one corpse and mutilated another. Security would be tightened.

Alistair drained his plastic cup and left without looking at anyone.

He saw a policeman and hurried away, up some stairs, along a corridor, turned left, turned right – going anywhere. He touched his stolen ID to a card reader and swung open a door into a darkened ward. Each little side room held a single patient. A nurse on the central desk stared at her computer screen and didn't look up.

Alistair ducked into one of the rooms.

The table was covered with cards and a helium balloon drooped on a ribbon. A handmade card said in childish lettering, *'Please get well Helena xxxx'*.

Helena was beautiful. Her long, dark hair lay plaited at the side of her head. She looked more than asleep. Tubes went into her nose and mouth, and a cobweb of wires joined her to monitors.

Excitement stirred in Alistair. Her hand was warm. He lifted it, touched the skin with his tongue and felt that electric thrill again. He remembered Ruby having a large red mark on her neck, long before they had become vampires.

'You can suck so hard you break blood vessels under the skin,' she'd said. 'Watch.' And she'd shown him how to do it on his own arm. He wanted to do it now to Helena.

He sucked harder and harder. He had the taste but not the blood.

Ignace had told them that vampires used to file

their teeth to points because biting through skin isn't easy. He'd already discovered that. Perhaps he would have to start filing his teeth. *You never see vampires doing that in movies,* he thought, *just like you never see people go to the loo, but they must do it.* 'All you need,' Ignace had said to them, 'is a puncture wound. A tiny hole – something you can suck from.'

That was what Alistair needed now.

He grabbed surgical scissors from a tray. His hand shook so much as he jabbed the pointed blade into the girl's arm that he sliced his own finger too. His blood leaked slowly, one or two drops mixing with hers. He lowered his mouth to the cut and sucked.

A noise startled him, but he couldn't stop, not

now. Someone was walking outside the door. He sucked harder, desperate to get all he could before it was too late.

At the click of the door handle he jerked his head away, and crouched beside the bed. A nurse walked in and looked at the monitors. Then her mouth opened in an 'O' shape as she saw Alistair.

She reached towards the alarm button by the bed, but he caught her ankle and dragged her to the ground. The nurse screamed once, and Alistair slapped his hand over her mouth and held it there.

'Shhhh.'

The woman kicked out, and tore open the back of his hand with her fingernails. She tried to scream, tried to bite him, but Alistair just pressed harder on her face.

He didn't dare let her go – she would scream. What if someone had heard her and was coming already?

The woman went limp. He pulled his hand away in horror. *Is she dead? She can't be dead!*

He scrabbled to his feet and ran out of the door. At the far end of the ward, two male nurses talked together. They looked up, and it took all the power Alistair could gather to walk slowly from the ward.

The men were already walking towards Helena's bed as the door to the ward closed behind him.

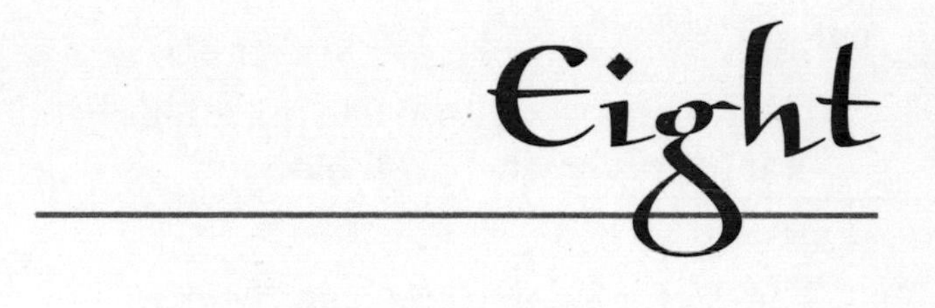

Eight

It was another hour before the doctor came back to the waiting room with a policewoman.

'Ruby. I'm sorry. The disappearance of the body seems to be part of a larger incident which the police are investigating. There's been another –' he glanced at the policewoman – 'another case involving a body.'

Ruby jumped up.

'What happened?'

The policewoman spoke first.

'It hasn't been made public. I'm afraid we can't tell you.'

'But it's my brother! You have to!'

The doctor ignored the policewoman.

'There are some marks on a body. We've increased security.'

The doctor and policewoman left her with the nurse again. Ruby felt sick with dread. What type of marks were on the body? She was sure she knew already. If Alistair was in the hospital, alive, he would need blood. It was a blessing if he had bitten only a dead person – so far. She had to find him before it got worse.

She told the nurse she was going to the Food Court, then walked the corridors, thinking and looking. What was Alistair wearing? Not his own clothes, so what? Where would he go? He'd go where he could hide, or where he could find blood.

She knew she should call Florence, their mentor, but still she held back. She didn't want trouble. Perhaps she could find him on her own. But she had to find him before the police did.

* * * * *

Alistair drifted back towards A&E. He didn't want to admit it to himself, but he knew he was being drawn there by the scent of blood. The few mouthfuls he'd taken would not keep him going for long.

He looked through the window of the double doors into the back entrance of A&E. There was a boy on a trolley, with a towel over his leg. Blood seeped through it in places, staining it red. The boy whimpered. But there were too many people near him.

'Excuse me,' someone said behind him. Alistair jumped back in alarm. A porter with a trolley wanted to go through the door. Alistair held it open for him, and looked down at two plastic pouches of deep red blood. Of course! Hospitals use blood all the time!

He looked back up the corridor the way the man had come and saw a door swinging. That must be the way to go to find blood.

Nine

Ruby's fingers tightened around the ProVamp capsule in her pocket. She could take it at any time, she didn't need to let things get too bad.

She was only six hours late with the capsule and already her body needed blood.

The only time she had felt this hunger before was when all this had started in the forest in Hungary, with Ava tied to the tree, when they first became vampires. She hated to remember it – how she had been completely overwhelmed by her need for blood.

How must Alistair be feeling? He'd not had ProVamp for nearly two days. But now she needed to feel what he felt – she needed that hunger for blood that he had, so that she would behave like him, so that it would lead her where it led him.

She tasted the air. There was something – a tang, a warmth almost – that drew her in one direction. She followed where it pulled her, back towards A&E.

Of course – that's where people would be bleeding. She hoped Alistair didn't go on a blood binge in A&E. There would be no explaining that away.

She crossed the waiting room and paused by the vending machine, pretending to decide what to buy, looking around. No one looked like Alistair.

She glanced at the TV screen on the wall. It showed a computer-generated picture of someone who could be Alistair, but in scrubs.

'Have you seen this man? Call hospital security,' it said underneath.

Her eyes were drawn to a man with a gash on his arm who had just walked in. The blood glistened. It was the most beautiful colour. She wanted to go over to him, just to be near.

A nurse called him into a side room, but even after he'd gone the scent of blood was left in the air. It was like a glittering snail trail that Ruby could have followed to the right room.

This was how it worked! This was how a vampire without ProVamp found blood. She realised now she could sense the blood in people around her even if they weren't bleeding.

An orderly pushed a trolley into the far end of the waiting room, while a young man in scrubs held the door for him. Ruby walked to the door and went through it before it swung shut, the young man hurrying away ahead of her.

Her phone beeped. She took it from her pocket and leaned against a wall, watched the man in scrubs disappear around a corner, and then clicked through to the message.

'Where are you both?'

It was from Florence, worried that she and Alistair hadn't checked in with her.

Ruby wouldn't be able to hide the fact that he was missing now. She had no idea what would happen. Would Ignace launch a full-scale search? Would she be in trouble? She hated the prospect of being in trouble with Ignace. She texted back that Alistair was in hospital but missing.

It was only as she put the phone back in her pocket that she realised. The man in front of her, the man in scrubs who had gone round the corner – he left no scent trail. He didn't smell of blood. There could be only one reason for that: he was a vampire. He was Alistair.

She ran along the corridor to the corner, but he'd gone. She'd been so close to him! But she couldn't track the lack of a scent.

Ruby stared down the empty corridor – door after door on either side, all closed, no doubt locked. She walked along, pushing on each door, pausing every time someone came past.

But then the smell of blood burst into her head like an explosion. This was nothing like the scent of a person, or even the clear tang of the blood in A&E. It was staggeringly intense – it made her reel and almost stumble.

She steadied herself against a wall and struggled with the tidal wave of hunger that crashed over her. She inched forward to the door she knew was the right one and pushed on it. It was locked.

'Alistair?' she whispered.

There was a tiny noise from inside – a wet noise.

'Alistair? It's Ruby.'

She felt the ProVamp in her fingers. She should take it now. No – she should give it to Alistair. Too late, though, surely?

That smell ... what was he doing? She hardly dared think about it. *Did he have a person in there?* She was both horrified and fascinated.

Did he have a person in there, and could she share the person?

Ten

'Alistair? Are you in there? Open the door.'

It opened a crack. Ruby's hand shook as she pushed on it – terrified of finding him in there with a corpse. Or – worse – not a corpse. And yet the taste of blood was driving her insane. She wanted to be in there too, whatever he was doing.

The door swung open. Alistair was huddled on the floor sucking blood from a pouch. *Like those yoghurt pouches we used to have in our school lunch-boxes* – the thought flashed through her head. He stared up at her, his eyes gleaming. He looked dazed, beyond all levels of happiness. An empty blood pouch lay on the floor beside him, and a pool of it had spilled onto the floor. Ruby longed to dip her fingers into it, even lick it from the floor.

'Alistair.' She held out the ProVamp capsule, hand trembling. He laughed.

'Why would I want that? This is so much better. Try it.' He held the pouch out to her.

Ruby was shaking violently now. She shook her head, but she didn't really mean *No*. She meant *YES* as loud as she could think it. She put the ProVamp into her own mouth and closed her eyes.

She would wait it out. Surely it could only take a minute or two and the capsule would work. She looked around, keeping her eyes off the blood.

They were in a storeroom, with racks of scrubs and boxes piled high in a corner.

'Where did you get that pouch?' she asked when the ProVamp kicked in. Alistair waved an arm towards the door.

'Out there,' he said. 'Blood room, next corridor. Do you want to get some?'

Alistair was acting as though he were drunk. He moved slowly, and blood dripped to the floor from the pouch in his hand.

'You have to get out of here,' Ruby said. As Alistair stood up, draining the last of the pouch, she saw that his scrubs were soaked in spilled blood.

'We need to get your clothes,' she added.

He smiled stupidly and pulled the jumper from its hiding place.

'I have this.'

'OK, it'll do. Take those off.' She turned her head away so that he could change – she knew he wouldn't do it otherwise.

Alistair screwed the scrubs into a ball and dropped them on the floor.

'Hide those,' Ruby said, pointing to the empty blood pouches. He dropped them behind the boxes where he'd hidden the jumper.

Ruby opened the door a crack. The corridor

was empty.

'I'll go first. I'll meet you in the Food Court.'

As he stood in front of her, blood ran in stripes down his legs and pooled on the floor, joining that he'd spilled. He just stared at her.

'What's the matter with you, Alistair?' she said. 'Go to a bathroom and wash that blood off before you go anywhere else. And pull yourself together – you're acting like a zombie. Is it the blood?'

He grinned at her, but didn't move.

Please do it right, she willed him, as she slipped out of the door.

Eleven

Ruby sat at a table in the Food Court with a black coffee and waited. Where was Alistair? How could it take so long?

She left her cup and walked back towards the storeroom. The corridor was swarming with police and was taped off at both ends. The door of the storeroom where she'd found Alistair was wide open. The blood-soaked scrubs were still lying on the floor. She had a little time, as the police wouldn't disturb them until the crime investigation team arrived – Ruby knew that. So they wouldn't find the blood pouches yet.

A line of bloody footprints led along the corridor, fading until there were just a few drops of blood, and then those stopped, too. It wasn't a trail to follow – at least, not for a human. She wished she hadn't taken the proVamp now. She needed still to be able to taste blood, to follow the trail to where Alistair washed it off.

The bathroom was just a few doors down on the left. Ruby dipped under the police tape and ran, hand over her mouth as though she would vomit.

'Stop!' shouted a policeman, running towards her.

'I'm going to be sick,' she shouted and pushed through the door. The policeman didn't follow, but waited outside.

One of the two cubicles was locked.

'Alistair?' she whispered. There was no answer. The sink was spattered with blood. She washed it away.

'Alistair, it's Ruby.' She crouched down and looked under the door. No feet. She went into the other cubicle and climbed onto the toilet so that she could look over the divider. Empty – but the window was open.

She went back into the corridor, mumbled thanks to the policeman and went back under the tape. He didn't move to stop her. And then she ran to the main door of the hospital and out, along the front and round the end of the building. She stumbled over scrubby grass, then past parked ambulances and bushes to where she thought the windows of the toilets should be.

'Alistair!' she called quietly. 'I'm here. Quick – you have to get out of here.'

Nothing. She called again, poked at the bushes, called a third time. And then she turned and saw the policeman.

'What's going on here?'

Ruby didn't know what to do.

'I'm looking for my brother.'

'Your brother? Isn't he the missing – body? Come on, love. Back into the hospital. Your brother isn't going to be out here. I'll get someone to see to you.'

'No – I don't want to go back. I need to walk on

my own. Just for a bit.'

'He's dead, you know. He's not going to be out here.'

'No. You're right. I was just – just hoping. Yes, please take me back inside.' She had to get the policeman away from where Alistair must be. Now she'd have to keep playing this crazy-with-grief card. She wished she'd been more careful.

'Yes,' she said loudly, in case Alistair was listening. 'Yes, officer, I'll come with you. Obviously there's no one here.'

* * * * *

Alistair waited in the bushes until Ruby and the policeman had left. He shivered. He didn't know the way home and he had nowhere to go.

He could run away. He imagined living out in the open, trying to find people to bite. Or he could go back inside. At least Ruby was inside.

After a few minutes, he crept out and wandered around until he found the main doors and walked in. There were police and security guards everywhere. They were on him in seconds, before he knew it, and bundled him into a room. Ruby was there. She ran over and hugged him.

'I told you he wasn't dead!' she cried. 'I could just feel he wasn't.'

The doctors wanted to examine Alistair.

'No! Don't touch me!' he shouted, raising his arms against them. Ruby held her breath; she knew the trouble it would cause if they discovered his low heartbeat and nearly undetectable breathing.

'He can refuse treatment,' she said. 'That's his right.'

They offered him food, which he didn't want. A nurse washed the dried blood from his legs, and Ruby was glad that she did as if they tested it they would find it wasn't his. That would not be good.

'We have some questions for you, too,' a policeman said. 'How did you get out of the morgue? And did you see a young man in green scrubs?'

Ruby squeezed Alistair's hand in warning.

'I saw lots of people in scrubs,' he said. 'The hospital is full of them. Why?'

'It's someone else we're looking for,' the policeman said.

'Was he dead too?'

'No. We want to question him. We can show you a picture ... '

'No!' Ruby said quickly. 'Not now. He needs to rest.' She knew if they looked at the picture they would realise Alistair was the man in scrubs.

The door opened and another doctor came in. She had short dark hair. She looked confident as she smiled at them.

'I'm Dr Karen Carew. You must be Ruby? We have a shared friend – Dr Ignace Guillotin. He suggested you might be more comfortable if I examined you, Alistair. Would that be all right?'

Alistair looked at Ruby; she nodded. A vampire doctor. She could tell by the smell of her – by the lack of smell – as well as by the reference to Ignace. Everything was going to be all right.

The policeman carried on.

'There was another body that was harmed. And a patient was hurt and a nurse was found unconscious. It's quite a coincidence, one body rising from the dead and another being mutilated on the same day ... '

'That really is a coincidence,' Dr Carew said firmly. 'My patient needs time to recover. You will be able to question him later, I'm sure.'

The policeman looked annoyed, but he shrugged and shook hands with Alistair.

'Welcome back to the land of the living.'

Epilogue

Upstairs in the coma unit, Helena stirred. She had not moved for three months. Her arm was bandaged, covering the wounds from her attack.

She groaned, and at the same time her vital signs dipped on the monitor and an alarm rang at the nurse station. Within seconds the room was full.

'Resus team!' a nurse called. 'She's flat-lining!'

But although the monitor showed she was dying, Helena sat up. She wrenched the monitor cable from her chest.

A nurse shook the heart monitor.

'Stupid thing. Either it's broken or she's the living dead.'

A doctor put a hand on Helena's arm.

'Shh. Slowly. You've been very ill.'

Helena looked at the veins on the back of the doctor's hand and opened her mouth. Her eyes gleamed. But she was weak, and had to lie back again.

For now.

Vampire Dawn

The story starts with ***Die Now or Live Forever****. Read it first.*

Then follow each individual's story. You can read these in any order:

Juliette's story

Finn's story

Omar's story

Alistair and Ruby's story

Ava's story

Plus an essential guide for new vampires.

Find out more at www.vampiredawn.co.uk. Follow the vampires on Facebook: www.facebook.com/VampireDawnBooks twitter: @vampiredawn